The second little pig also liked to sing and play. He built a ramshackle little house from sticks.

But the third little pig, who was *very* wise—and not lazy—built a strong house of bricks.

"I'll be safe and you'll be sorry when the wolf comes to your door," said the third little pig. He knew that nothing was as safe and strong as bricks—and wolf-proof paint!

But his brothers just laughed and headed merrily down the forest path, not worried at all.

"If we see the Big Bad Wolf, we'll punch him in the nose! Why, we'll kick him in the shins!" said those two little pigs.

And who should be listening. . . but the Big Bad Wolf! When the pigs saw the wolf, they turned tail and ran for home.

Trembling and shivering, the first little pig pulled in the welcome mat of his straw house and slammed the door!

"Open the door and let me in," cried the Big Bad Wolf.

"Not by the hair on my chinny-chin-chin," squealed the pig.

"Then I'll huff and puff and blow your house in!"

And he did!

The little pig ran—all the way to his brother's house of sticks.

The two pigs thought they were safe, so they sang and danced around merrily.

But the wolf had a plan! He covered himself in a sheepshin and squeaked, "Little pigs, little pigs, let me in!"

"Not by the hairs of our chinny-chin-chins!" cried the two pigs.

"Then I'll huff and puff and blow your house in!" And he did!

The two little pigs ran—all the way to their brother's house of bricks.

"I told you this would happen," the third pig said. "But now you're safe and sound."

Inside, the third little pig played a happy little jig. Outside, the wolf huffed and puffed and huffed and puffed—but the brick house didn't move an inch.

"Why, I'll just climb down the chimney," laughed the Big Bad Wolf.

"Oh, my!" said the third little pig. "He's on the roof!" And he rushed to pull the lid off the pot of boiling water, and. . .

. . .down came the Big Bad Wolf—*splash!*—right into that pot of hot water!

Then up, up, up shot the wolf—clear out of the chimney!

The Big Bad Wolf galloped down the road as fast as his legs could carry him—and he never bothered the three little pigs again.